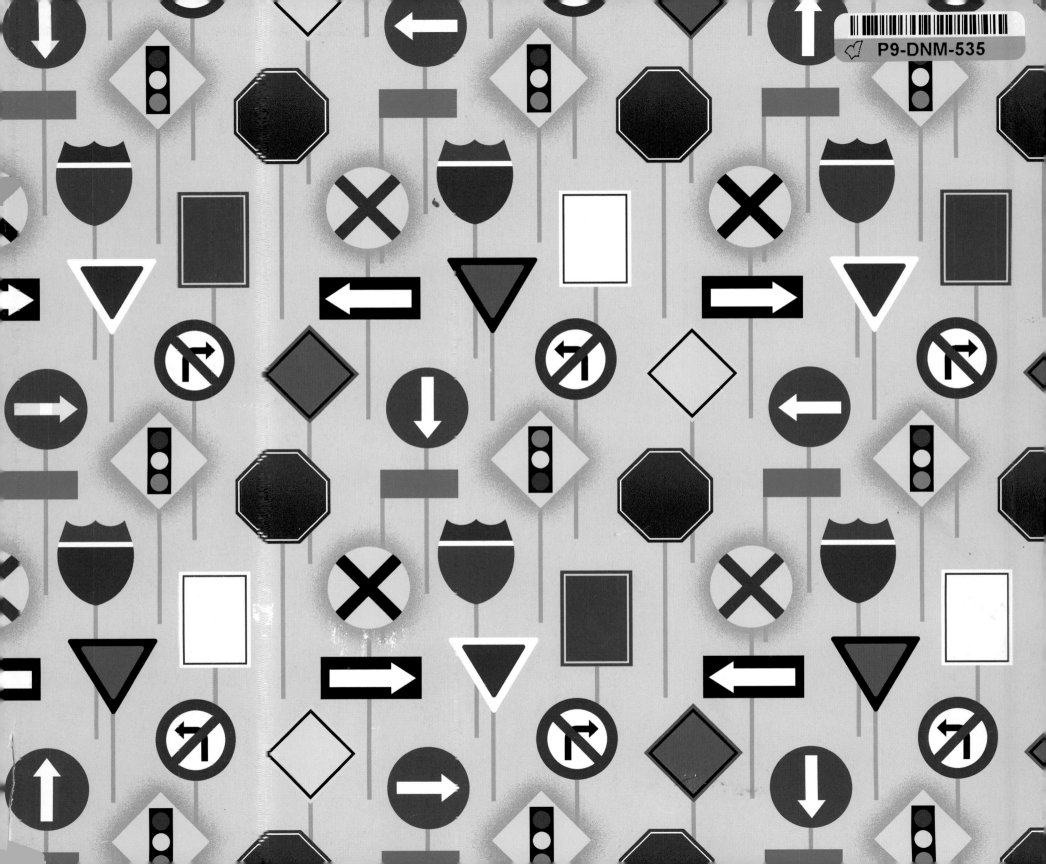

THE RUNAWAY NO-WHEELER

by **Peter Stein** illustrated by **Bob Staake**

VIKING

TONY was a rugged truck who had a lot to haul.
He'd load his rig and hit the road
without a hitch or stall.

LOADING DOCK

CAUTION

That truck was strong, super fast,
and always right on time.
But then one day **DISASTER** struck . . .

when Tony slipped on slime!
He swerved and slid and with a skid
on gooey globs of green,
Tony, who had **18** wheels . . .

DANGER: CLIFF

POP!

now had **17**.

The road ahead was **AWFUL.**
Tony bumped and bounced.
"I f-feel I'll lose another w-wheel!"
the troubled truck announced.

BETTER ROADS

FOOD

WIFI

GAS

Then the driving got much **WORSE**—
the street was split and cracked!

Then **BING!** and **BOING!**

MORE wheels lost!
(**2**, to be exact.)

Tony drove on **15** wheels along the countryside,
until he saw a mama duck—
"with BABIES!" Tony cried.

Thinking fast, and with a blast,
he jumped above the chicks.
And when he landed—

BOOM!

He'd lost wheels **4!** And **5!** And **6!**

Tony had a job to do—
there was no turning back.

He clenched his grille and drove along,
straight into . . .

THE BLACK.

Tony felt a painful YANK! caused by pulling pliers!

And just like that, a gang of thieves had stolen **3 MORE TIRES!**

9 WHEELS GONE! 9 WHEELS LEFT!
But Tony never stopped.
On he went, a charging truck
that wobbled, waved, and hopped!

Bruised but strong,
he cruised along
and kept a steady
pace, then with a . . .

SMASH!

he somehow struck . . .
a **ROCKET SHIP** from space!

ALIENS swarmed the truck! They gobbled up **5 WHEELS!**
"Thank you, earthling," said their king. "We eat wheels for meals."

Tony almost lost control. How could this go on?
Could he drive with **4** wheels left . . .
and **14** tires gone?

DANGER: CURVY ROADS

ONE WAY

"I MUST," he said. "I CAN," he cried, weaving down the road.
"I'M on time, EVERY time. I. Will. Bring. My. LOAD!"

And then . . . **OH NO.** A nut popped off.
A gear. A spring. A screw.
This crazy trip had jarred them loose!
What would Tony *do*?

"YIKES!" he yelled. **"3 MORE** wheels gone! Now I have just **1!**
I'm out of whack and can't hold back—

HELP!

LOOK OUT!

RUN!!!"

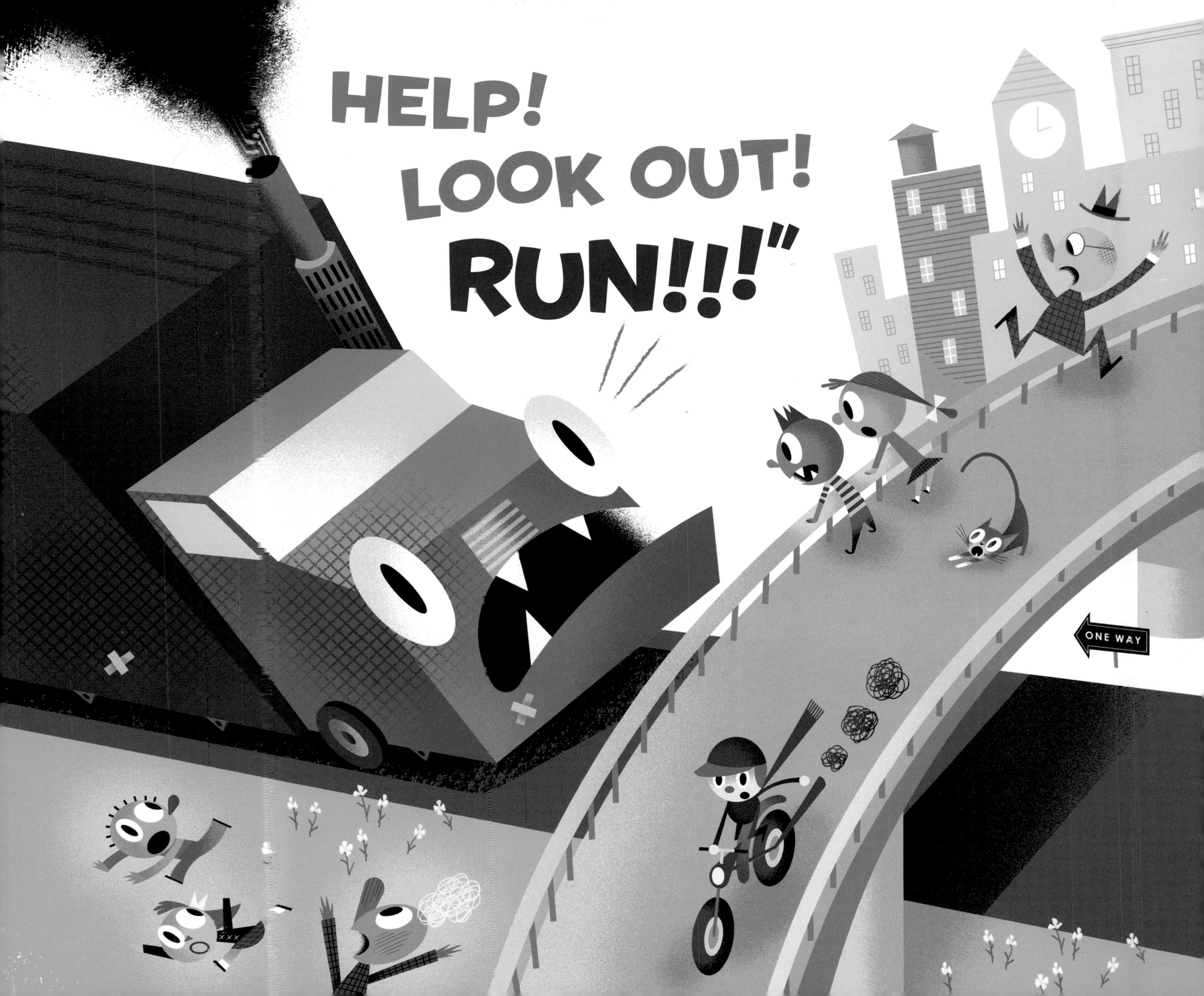

"But wait," he gasped, about to crash.
"Can it really be?
Up ahead—the building where
I'll make DELIVERY!"

His destination now in sight,
Tony felt an urge.
"I'll try my HARDEST," said the truck—
and made a mighty **SURGE.**

Almost at the finish line,
Tony hit a trough.
And then a wheel . . .
his **FINAL** wheel . . .
silently . . .
fell off.

NINCOMPOOP
PLUMBING FIXTURES

Drink
Burpo!
SODA

BUMFUZZLE INDUSTRIES

You might think, *Well, that's the end.*
Tony's out of luck.
But Tony didn't think that way. . . .
That dude is one tough truck.

As his **18TH** wayward wheel
landed who-knows-where,
Tony hit the gas and leaped,
flying through the air.

MONKEY
CITY

"Where Everyone Shops For Monkeys."

PIZ
POPSIC

WE DELIVE

After all those thrills and chills and hills he had to climb . . . fluffy chicks and awful thieves and aliens and slime . . .

HUG A FROG DAY
June 6
MARK THE DATE!

PUCKLEPICKLE
BUILDING

WAREHOUSE
DELIVERIES

WESTERN
LOADING ZONE

after losing all his wheels, and
caked in grease and grime . . .
Tony landed, loud and proud . . .

SKREEEEI

"YES!" exclaimed the tired truck.
"I'm *finally* off the road.
And now, to end a hard day's work . . .

"I'll **DUMP** this heavy load!"

For Lonnie, Rory, and Travis—P. S.

For Elliot Handler, the inventor of Hot Wheels—B. S.

VIKING
An imprint of Penguin Random House LLC, New York

First published in the United States of America by Viking, an imprint of Penguin Random House LLC, 2020
Text copyright © 2020 by Peter Stein
Art copyright © 2020 by Bob Staake

Visit us online at penguinrandomhouse.com

LIBRARY OF CONGRESS CATALOGING-IN-PUBLICATION DATA IS AVAILABLE.
ISBN 9780593114209

Manufactured in China

1 3 5 7 9 10 8 6 4 2

The art for this picture book was created using a combination of pens, brushes, crayons, charcoal, and ink spatters—
and by drawing with a handheld mouse in Adobe Photoshop 3.0.

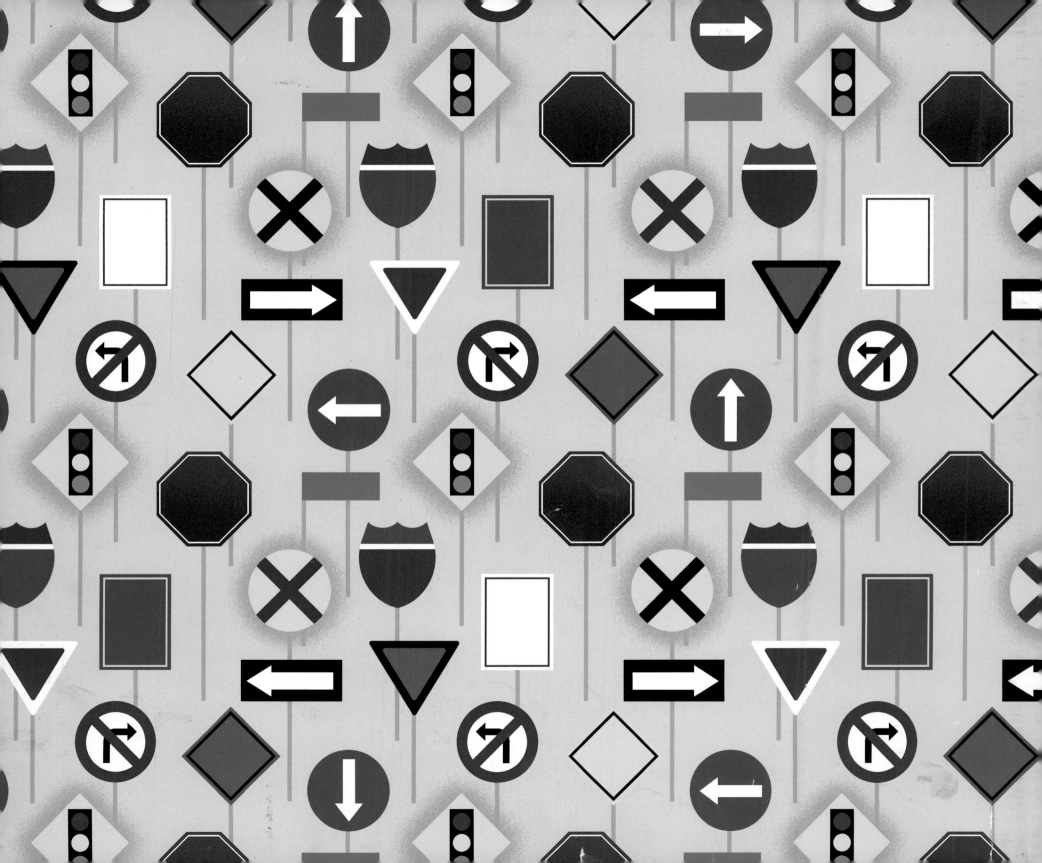